# MEGA ★BUNNY

MEGA BEAR

MOSQUITO MAN

MEGA PIG

MEGA CROC

MEGA PANDA

MEGA HIPPO

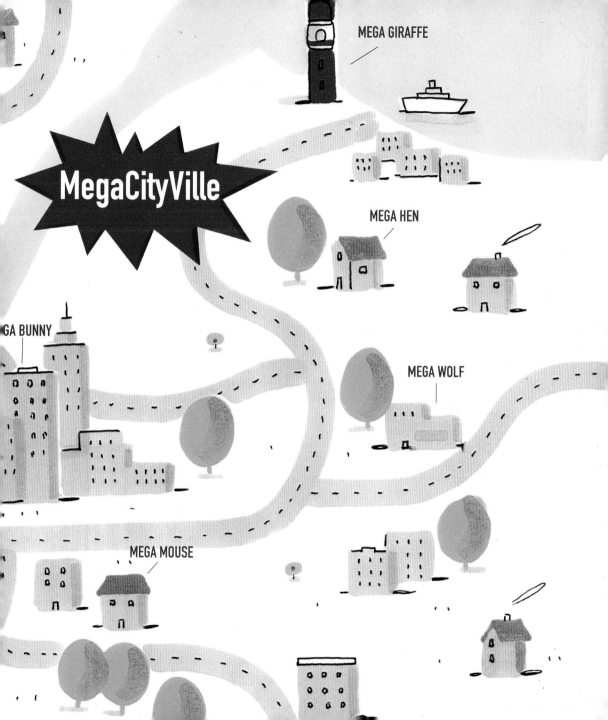

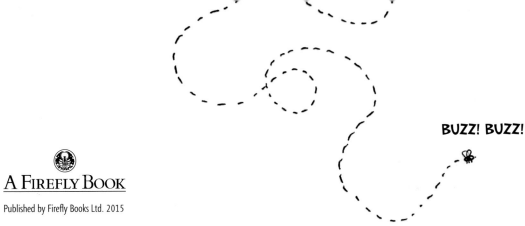

BUZZ! BUZZ!

# A FIREFLY BOOK

Published by Firefly Books Ltd. 2015

Illustrations copyright © 2014 Mango Jeunesse, Paris
English translation copyright © 2015 Firefly Books

First printing

**Publisher Cataloging-in-Publication Data (U.S.)**

A CIP record for this title is available from the Library of Congress

**Library and Archives Canada Cataloguing in Publication**

A CIP record for this title is available from Library and Archives Canada

Published in the United States by
Firefly Books (U.S.) Inc.
P.O. Box 1338, Ellicott Station
Buffalo, New York 14205

Published in Canada by
Firefly Books Ltd.
50 Staples Avenue, Unit 1
Richmond Hill, Ontario L4B 0A7

Printed in China

# MEGA ★ BUNNY

**SÉVERINE VIDAL**

**BARROUX**

## How Mega Bunny
## hopped onto the moon

FIREFLY BOOKS

This is Mega Bunny.
He has, like all the other bunnies,
long ears, soft fur and
a small round tail.

little spoon

Mega Bunny poop

He lives way up there, on the top floor of MegaCityVille's giant tower.

On the roof, he takes care of his garden where he grows...carrots!

Because, like all bunnies,
Mega Bunny loves:

carrot soup

Did you happen
to see my little
spoon?

carrot juice

carrot puree

carrot cake

Sometimes, between two carrot meals, Mega Bunny must save the world from the dreadful **Mosquito Man**, the Big Wicked Mosquito thirsty for blood.

For that, he puts on his Mega boots, so his hops will become Mega hops.

He Mega hops over the clouds,
he Mega hops over the buildings,
**he Mega hops over everything.**

In short, let's say that Mega Bunny likes to eat and is very disorganized.
He jumps very high and very far.

Everyone in town dreams of having a Mega Bunny at home.

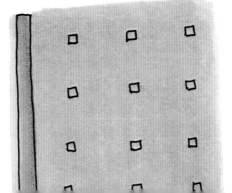

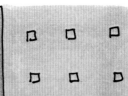

Today, Mega Bunny is spending his day at home with all his friends.

Suddenly, he notices the warning signal in the sky. Someone needs Mega Bunny!

Another of the dreadful
**Mosquito Man's** dirty tricks!

Look! Tom Thumb is stuck on the Moon!

Tom Thumb will have to wait a little longer:
Mega Bunny is the most disorganized of the Mega Animals.
And that's annoying.
He's always losing everything...

...his keys, his tooth brush, **his wallet, his underpants**...

And even his boots!

That's it! Mega Bunny has found
his Mega boots.

He puts them on very fast and jumps like a giant
in the direction of the Moon.
A magnificent Mega Bunny hop!

Mega Bunny is incredible.
It's amazing, it looks like he's flying.
# What a show!

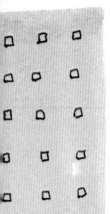
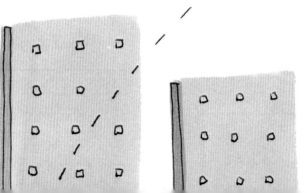

There's no object too high for Mega Bunny!

Mega Bunny takes action as soon as he lands on the Moon.
He's afraid of nothing!

Mega Bunny fights with courage against the evil
**Mosquito Man** and crushes him instantly.

He gets Tom Thumb back: phew!
The horrifying Mosquito Man is
already far away!

Mega Bunny has fulfilled his mission and he is very tired!
He has earned a good sleep.

But when Mega Bunny goes to bed,
he needs his night light.

Shhh...it's a secret!

MEGA BEAR

MOSQUITO MAN

MEGA PIG

MEGA CROC

MEGA PANDA

MEGA HIPPO

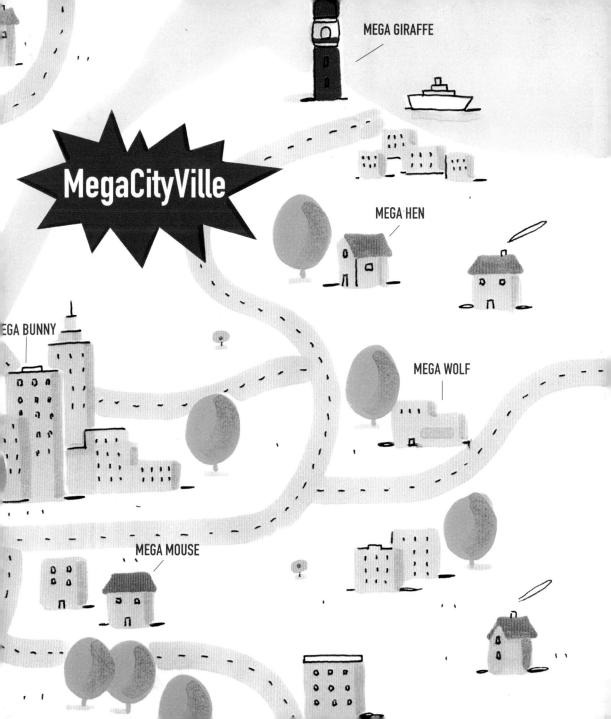